SNOW FAMILY

by Daniel Kirk

Hyperion Books for Children

NEW YORK

Whoosh! blows the northern wind,
"CAW!" laughs the crow.
Crunch! go the little boots
on fresh-fallen snow.

Zing! spins the snowball—
throw one if you dare.
Snow children are not afraid
to tease a sleepy bear.

"You dropped your scarf," the sparrow scolds.
"Where did you lose your nose?
You wild children ought to be
more careful with your clothes!"

But not a single snow child
cares what the sparrow said,
for a family builds a snow boy
in the field just ahead.

"BRRR!" shivers Jacob,
who holds the snow boy's cap.
His father fastens Jacob's coat,
snap, snap, snap.

His mother tightens Jacob's scarf.
She gives his cheek a pat,
and a kiss upon his little nose,
just like that!

Ooo-wooh! speeds the chilly wind
across the frozen land,
where a child of snow may come to life
and join a wandering band.

Waiting in the dairy barn,
the cattle bellow, "MOOO!"
On a farm there're lots of chores
a little boy can do.

"WOOF! WOOF!" Jacob's dog barks
like he's never barked before.
Jacob puts his bucket down
and peers around the door.

"Don't go," frets the squirrel,
"where a boy does not belong!"
"Follow," sings the cardinal,
"for your heart is never wrong!"

Clomp! Clomp! go his little feet,
for Jacob's got to roam.
He goes to meet new playmates
in the forest far from home.

Crash and *rumble*, *romp* and *bumble*,
snowballs dash against a tree.
Stomp and *fumble*, *smash* and *tumble*,
how they play, so recklessly!

Jacob frowns. "You lost your glove.
You tore your hat. It isn't right!
You need someone to care for you.
Who tucks you in at night?"

But all the little ones have mischief
on their minds again.
They're bound to wake the grumpy bear
who's sleeping in his den!

Zing! Zing! rush the snowballs,
whizzing through the air.
"Run away!" the rabbit warns.
"GRRRR!" growls the bear.

The frightened children run to hide,
they scurry to and fro.
Jacob dashes for a tree
across the frozen snow.

Huff! Puff! Up the tree he climbs.
But can a bear climb, too?
Little feet slip on a branch,
and off comes Jacob's shoe.

Just then a shout comes from the woods.
The brown bear turns to flee.
Jacob's mom and dad arrive,
and lift him from the tree.

His mother tightens Jacob's scarf.
She gives his cheek a pat,
and a kiss upon his little nose,
just like that!

"Jacob!" calls the winter wind. "Tomorrow," chirp the wrens, "you must come back and build snow parents for your friends!"

The next day, while the children
watch, in the field below,
Jacob builds a mother and
a father from the snow.

With legs to lead the little ones,
and arms to hold them tight,
with mittens, hats, and coal-black eyes,
they sparkle with delight.

Snow parents tighten every scarf.
They give each cheek a pat,
and a kiss on every carrot nose,
just like that!

for Ken and Sylvia Marantz

First Edition
1 3 5 7 9 10 8 6 4 2

Printed in Hong Kong by South China Printing Company Ltd.

Library of Congress Cataloging-in-Publication Data
Kirk, Daniel
Snow family / by Daniel Kirk.—1st ed.
p. cm.
Summary: A young boy decides to build a snow family to take care of his snow boy the way his parents take care of him.
ISBN: 0-7868-0304-5 (trade: alk. paper)
ISBN: 0-7868-2244-9 (library: alk. paper)
[1. Snowmen—Fiction. 2. Parent and child—Fiction. 3. Stories in rhyme.] I. Title.
PZ8.3.K6553Sn 2000
[E]—dc21   98-51079

The author wishes to thank Howard Reeves and Ken Geist
for their sensitive and insightful help in editing the manuscript of this book.